MELODY & CORREL

STACEY RIDDELL

Illustrated by Stacey Riddell, Caitlin Lehman, Ashley Woods & Tristan Hummel

KidzVerse, LLC

Chicago

Special Thanks To:

Joseph, Sharon & Lauren Flowers
Glenn, Marla, Henry & Jacob Primack
Naomi Gitlin
Peak6
Patrick McCoy
John Franczyk
Patrick Rubey
Andy Verb
Spencer Connaughton
Maria Squeri

Published by KidzVerse, LLC
© 2007 KidzVerse, LLC

For information regarding permission, contact:
KidzVerse, LLC
1147 West Ohio Street, Suite 204
Chicago, Illinois 60622
contact@kidzverse.com

Learn more about KidzVerse at www.kidzverse.com

Library of Congress control number: 2007908051
ISBN 978-0-9800937-4

Printed in Melrose Park, Illinois by Lake Book Manufacturing, Inc.

Melody, a beautiful hippo with a big green bow, lives along a river in the savannah of Africa. She reads for hours, sometimes out loud to the other animals.

Each book Melody reads is filled with different animals in faraway places that she later sings about.

♪ Hippos to the left, zebras to the right
Monkeys in the middle, birds out of sight
They read and play all day
And sing and dance all night
Animals, beautiful animals
Makin' the world so bright ♪

One day, after Melody
finishes singing, she looks
through her basket of books. Suddenly,
she hears a jazzy voice coming from the tree.

A grey blur shoots out of the leaves!
It whirls, twirls and zigzags through the air with amazing speed!

"Girl, you have got a VOICE! Who are you?" asks the bird as he stops in mid-air.

"I'm Melody!"

"Niiiice! My name is Correl, the oxpecker. I love music but never heard that song before. Is it yours?"

Melody takes out the book she was singing the song about.
Correl lands on Melody's shoulder and looks into the book with excitement.

"Wow, is that place for real? Somewhere I can jam?" Correl asks.

"I hope so, all those animals look really happy there!" Melody replies.

Correl jumps off of Melody's shoulder onto a tree stump.
"Maybe we can go there someday. I can watch over
you and we can have fun together," he says with a smile.

Melody asks her new friend,
Correl, if he knows how to dance.

"If you do, we can sing and dance
together at the gigantic party
the animals have to welcome the
rainy season to the savannah."

Correl promises to practice with Melody every day until the big event.

One day, the two rest after practicing for hours. Correl blurts out, "It's getting hotter and that river is looking more and more like a Correl-sized swimming pool."

"I hope it rains soon," Melody says.
"We need water to live."

After many hot days with no rain in sight, the animals decide to pack their things and look for a new place to live where there is more water.

Every night, the animals camp together under the stars and moon.
Melody reads softly to them as they fall asleep.

One night, Melody tells Correl she is scared and asks, "What if we don't find water?"

Correl tries to comfort Melody, "Don't worry Mel, we'll find water soon!"

The next day when the animals are hiking, a tiny wild dog at the back of the pack points to the sky and shouts, "Hey, wait everyone! Look over there! Clouds!"

"The rain! It has finally come!" the animals cheer.

"Nooo! It's a sandstorm!"
All the animals scatter in the wind and sand.

Melody reaches up to make sure Correl is still beside her. Correl points to some caves they can use for shelter.

As Melody and Correl enter the cave,
the wind pulls her green bow off
her head. By the time the two of them
turn to grab the bow, it's gone!

They watch the other animals run for shelter.

"We'll find your bow when the wind stops blowing," Correl says to Melody.

"I hope so, that was my special green bow. It's magical," Melody whispers.

Tired and thirsty, they eventually fall asleep thinking how lucky they are to have each other.

A new sound wakes Melody and Correl.
It's like nothing they have ever heard before.

Suddenly, two funny looking animals
wrapped in cloth and without any
fur appear outside the cave.

The two funny looking animals cool off Melody and Correl after giving them water to drink.

Melody and Correl are put onto
a plane where they quickly fall asleep.

Melody wakes up in a new place. She checks all around but no Correl!
At that moment, she hears sounds coming from a few feet away.

A door opens and in comes one of the funny looking animals carrying Correl.
"Correl!" Melody shouts.

Correl does loop-de-loops in the air and screams excitedly,
"Melody, you're here! Yeaaaah!"

The funny looking animals take good care of Melody and Correl.

"Where are we?" Melody asks Correl.

"The Zoo!" he replies.

They talk about how great The Zoo is, but wonder where their old friends are.

"We should sing our song from the savannah," Melody says.

"Yeah! If our friends hear us they will come out!" Correl yells.

They start to sing and dance.

Wondering if the animals will be able to hear her, Melody climbs onto the highest rock she can find. She starts to sing, louder and louder and louder.

"Our old friends from the savannah are here! They heard your singing and came out!"
Correl shouts to Melody.

Melody climbs down to join the others who are singing and dancing joyously.

"Hooray! Hooray! We're all together at The Zoo!"

When the singing and dancing stops, Correl gives Melody a brand new pink bow to match the color on her belly.

Melody thanks Correl who blushes and says, "That's what friends are for."

Melody loves her new bow but still thinks about her old one.

That night, Melody dreams of how she
found the magical green bow along the riverbank in the savannah.
It was in a small wooden box with a note inside: *The one who finds this will be protected!*

Melody hopes whoever finds the bow will be safe and happy just like she and Correl are.

To find out more about the animals and the magical bow, visit www.kidzverse.com